The
Bug
Collector

For Anna, for all your help and support from beginning to end. And for Amelia and George, my bug collectors.

American edition published in 2020
by Andersen Press USA,
an imprint of Andersen Press Ltd.
www.andersenpressusa.com

First published in Great Britain in 2019 by
Andersen Press Ltd., 20 Vauxhall Bridge Road, London SW1V 2SA.

Distributed in the United States and Canada by Lerner Publishing Group, Inc.
241 First Avenue North, Minneapolis, MN 55401 USA
For reading levels and more information, look up this title at www.lernerbooks.com.

Color separated in Switzerland by Photolitho AG, Zürich.
Printed and bound in China.

Library of Congress Cataloging-in-Publication Data Available
ISBN: 978-1-5415-9634-4
eBook ISBN: 978-1-5415-9635-1

1 –TOPPAN–9/1/19

The Bug Collector

Alex G. Griffiths

A

ANDERSEN PRESS USA

Today was George's favorite
day of the whole week.
It was Sunday, and that
meant that he was going on
an adventure with Grandad.

This particular Sunday, Grandad took George to . . .

...the Museum of Wildlife!
Inside, they saw ferocious dinosaurs,

wondrous whales,

massive mammoths, and
even stranger creatures of
every color and shape.

INSECT WORLD →

Chop chop, Georgie!

SO COOL!

But Grandad didn't stop to look at any of it.
He was too excited about something completely different . . .

WOW!

The creatures he wanted to show George were
much smaller and stranger, and Grandad loved them.

On the journey home, George could think of nothing else but the marvelous bugs he had seen that day.

That night, George's dreams were filled with buzzing
bees, floating butterflies, and sliding snails.

When he woke up, George couldn't wait to get outside.

SO EXCITED!

He packed his backpack and headed
out to see what he could find.

In the garden, he noticed
bugs everywhere!

Something fluttered
past George's face.

He tried to catch it . . .

...but it was too quick for him!

Catching bugs was not as easy as George had thought.

They were so clever. They always seemed to know what he was going to do.

George had to learn to be even more
clever to outwit them.

Soon, he was a master bug catcher!

With his backpack and cart loaded up,
George set off for his treehouse.

After he'd found a place
for every bottle and jar,
George admired his collection.

Examining them closely, he saw so many
different shapes and colors.

As George went home for dinner,
everything seemed silent and still.

Nothing

buzzed,

fluttered

or scuttled.

IT'S SO QUIET...

The next day, he went back
to the garden to continue the hunt.

But everywhere was dull and sad.

Grandad also wondered what was going on.

He knew something didn't seem right.

Suddenly, Grandad realized: all the bugs had gone!

Back at the treehouse, George looked at
his collection. The bugs didn't look happy.

Grandad wasn't happy either when he
saw what George had been doing.

He loved bugs as much as George, but knew that
living ones shouldn't be kept in jars and bottles.

Grandad explained to George the important jobs
bugs have in the outside world, especially in our gardens.

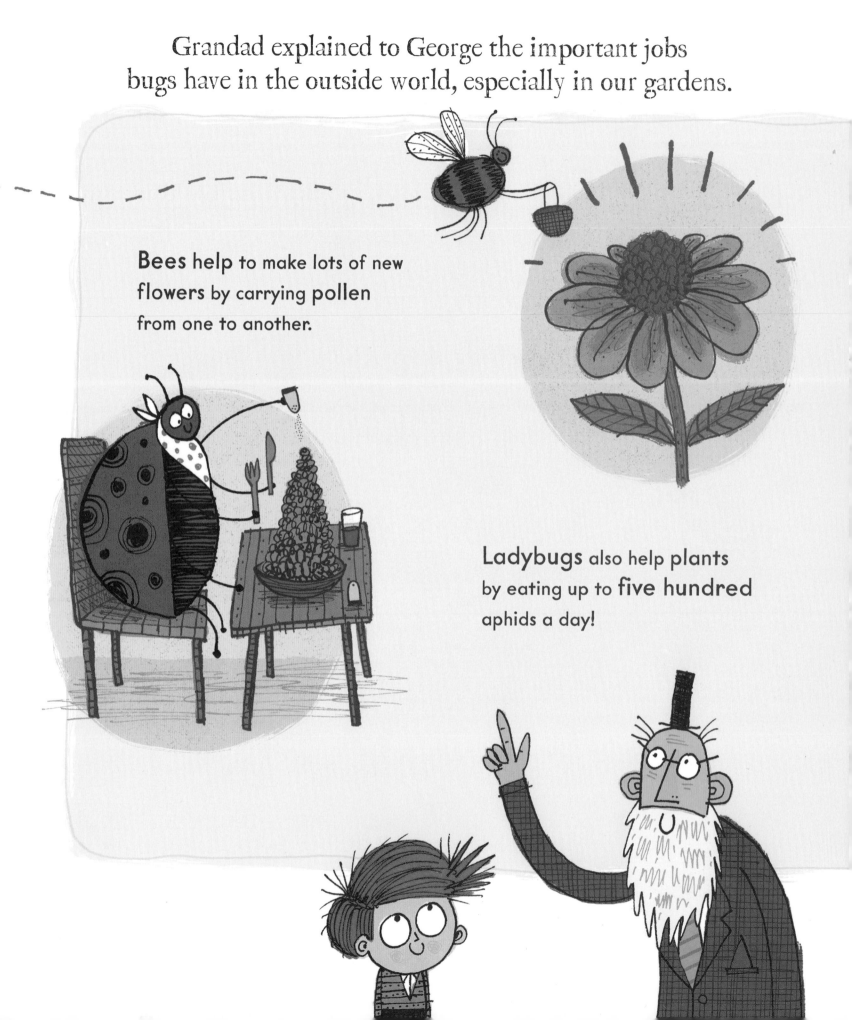

Bees help to make lots of new
flowers by carrying **pollen**
from one to another.

Ladybugs also help plants
by eating up to **five hundred**
aphids a day!

Ants are natural farmers, carrying seeds and planting them in new places.

Dung beetles turn waste into food!

And of course, all insects are an important part of the natural food chain. If we take them away, lots of animals won't get their dinner.

George listened carefully. He knew what he had to do.

He opened the jars,
the bottles, the windows
and doors, and the
bugs flew out.

The sky was alive again!

George was sad to see them go.

But Grandad was smiling. He had an idea . . .

It took a little while, but together, they changed the garden into a bug sanctuary to share with everyone.

George's Great BIG Bug World

Grandad and George
agreed that watching bugs in
their natural habitat was the
very best thing in the world.